Sumn

Story Keeper Series
Book 16

Dave and Pat Sargent (*left*) are longtime residents of Prairie Grove, Arkansas. Dave, a fourth-generation dairy farmer, began writing in early December of 1990. Pat, a former teacher, began writing in the fourth grade. They enjoy the outdoors and have a real love for animals.

Sue Rogers (*right*) returned to her beloved Mississippi after retirement. She shared books with children for more than thirty years. These stories fulfill a dream of writing books—to continue the sharing.

Summer Milky Way

Story Keeper Series
Book 16

By Dave and Pat Sargent
and Sue Rogers

Beyond "The End"
By Sue Rogers

Illustrated by Jane Lenoir

Ozark Publishing, Inc.
P.O. Box 228
Prairie Grove, AR 72753

Cataloging-in-Publication Data

Sargent, Dave, 1941–
    Summer Milky Way / by Dave and
Pat Sargent and Sue Rogers ; illustrated by
Jane Lenoir. —Prairie Grove, AR : Ozark
Publishing, c2005.
        p. cm. (Story keeper series ; 16)

    "Be compassionate"—Cover.
    SUMMARY: Ahiga was destined to be a
special person. When he found a buffalo
stone, his parents understood what Spider God
had said on his visit.
        ISBN 1-56763-933-X (hc)
               1-56763-934-8 (pbk)

    1. Indians of North America—Juvenile
fiction. 2. Blackfeet Indians—Juvenile fiction.
[1. Native Americans—United States—Fiction.
2. Blackfeet Indians—Fiction.] 1. Sargent,
Pat, 1936– II. Rogers, Sue, 1933– III. Lenoir,
Jane, 1950– ill. IV. Title. V. Series

    PZ7.S243Su 2005
    [Fic]—dc21   2003090098

Inspired by

black moccasins dyed with prairie fire ash.

Dedicated to

storytellers, past and present, who weave our literary heritage into intriguing tales.

Foreword

Spider God climbed down the summer Milky Way to tell a Blackfeet father that his expected son would be a special person. The baby was named Ahiga. His father taught Ahiga to be a hunter and warrior. But when Ahiga found a buffalo stone, his father asked the holy man to help with Ahiga's training to be a buffalo caller.

Contents

If you would like to have the authors of the Story Keeper Series visit your school, free of charge, just call us at 1-800-321-5671 or 1-800-960-3876.

One

My Father's Hands

The first rays of morning sun shone through the doorway into the big tipi circle of our village. The warmest rays found the doorway to my father's tipi. I lay in my father's arms, his newborn son.

"Good morning, Ahiga," Father said, speaking my name for the first time. "Spider God climbed down the summer Milky Way to tell me of your coming. He brought me your name. I have held it in my heart through the long, cold winter. Now I give it to you, Ahiga. It means he fights."

1

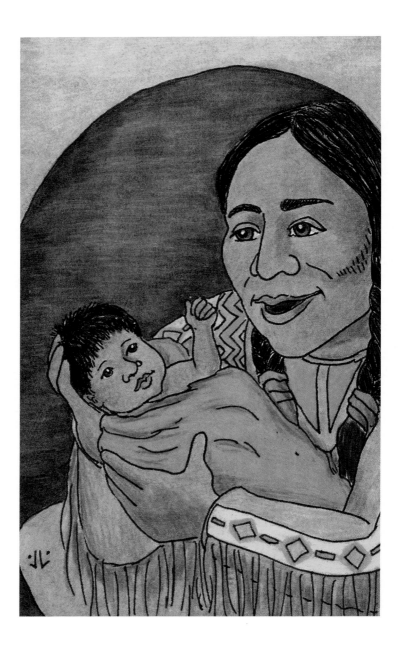

"You, my tiny ohko (son), will be a brave patron of warriors. You will grow sturdy and wise and will take your place among our people. You must learn to be compassionate and kind." My father talked for a long time. His warm breath was like a blanket, bonding me to his strong hands.

Father's hands provided everything his family needed. They were sure and powerful. They could sink an arrow into a buffalo up to the feather. My father rode within a bow's length to the buffalo. Any closer would have brought him into hooking range. Out came an arrow from his quiver, the nock hooked on the bowstring—ready. His target was just behind the buffalo's last rib, in back of the left shoulder—straight

into the heart. Never were two of my
father's arrows found in a buffalo!

The buffalo provided food and clothing, shelter, tools, and utensils for our family.

Even from my cradleboard, I watched Father's hands chipping arrowheads and smoothing shafts. His hands were careful. They made good teachers.

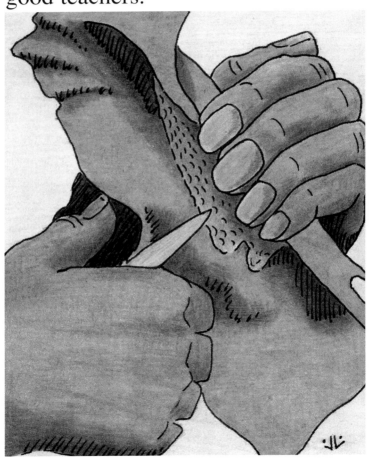

I could make my own arrows by the time I had seen five winters.

"Come, Son," said my father one day. "It is time you learned to ride a horse. A good warrior and hunter must be a skillful rider."

Father taught me many things. He showed me how to tie a buffalo robe on my horse with a buckskin cinch. He told me to strip to a clout to reduce my weight and to free my movements.

"Hunting is close to warfare, my son," said Father. "You and your horse must have cool nerves. You must have sharp reflexes to catch up with and get away from a stampeding herd. If your horse cannot run down a buffalo in a short time, you will not have a successful hunt."

My father gave me one of his finest yearling ponies, a red roan mustang. His tail started out white and ended in black. His mane and tail were very long. He had a dorsal stripe that had many shades of color.

"His name is Blaze, because of the white mark on his face," I said.

From that day, Blaze was my responsibility. Father taught me to ride with strength and speed. Blaze taught me gentleness. Father taught me how to make commands for Blaze through my knees and a rawhide thong tied to his lower jaw. Blaze taught me self-reliance.

"A hunter needs both hands free in war and in the chase," said Father. "Drop the reins on your horse's neck or hold them in your teeth."

Blaze learned to stop instantly at a nudge of my knees or from a tug on the rawhide thong, called a war bridle. He had to learn not to shy or buck whenever he came close to buffalo. My father said to teach him to trust me. Then he would race through a confusion of buffalo, dust, and noise.

"You and your horse are doing well, my son," said Father. "It is time you learned to make a rope. It must be long enough to reach from my door to your grandfather's door."

"Why do I need such a long rope, Father?" I asked.

"You'll see," answered Father.

Two

Buffalo Stone

My friends and I rode our ponies, explored the plains, raced across the grassland, and had pretend wars and hunts! We sometimes had luck in our hunts. My father was always pleased when I brought home small game. He wanted to hear all about how I captured the animal.

"How is Blaze doing? Is he learning your commands?" he asked.

"Yes, Father. He is learning to stop fast. He stopped so fast today that I slid right off his back," I said. "But look, Father. This was under a large clump of prairie grass. I would not have seen it if I had not landed flat in the dirt!" I held out my hand to show Father my treasure.

My father's face changed from one expression to another. He looked at my mother and motioned her to come to us.

"Show your mother, my young son," Father said.

Mother looked at my open hand. She took a quick breath.

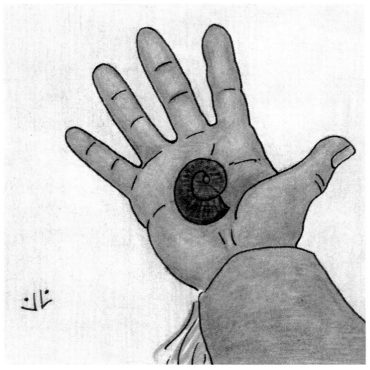

15

What had I done? What was wrong with this rock? It was shaped like a buffalo. I thought they would be pleased!

"Has the rock made a noise, Ahiga?" asked my mother.

"Yes, Mother. I think it chirped like a bird when it lay on the ground," I said. "But it has not made a sound since."

"We believe you have found a special stone, an Iniskim," said Father. "Protect it at all times. It has much power. Put it in your medicine bundle. Before the next sun shines in our doorway, ride Blaze out onto the prairie. Take four rattles and your stone. Listen to the stone. Tell us what happens."

The next morning, before the sun peeped over the prairie grass,

Blaze and I rode far away from the tipi village.

Suddenly a clear voice sang out. *"The buffalo will all drift back. The buffalo will all drift back."*

The voice was coming from my medicine bundle. It was the buffalo stone. I nudged Blaze to stop. I took the stone out and held it in my hand. It still looked the same, but it was singing. Everything it said was a song. It pointed out a buffalo chip and told me to ride a short distance away. Then I was told to shake the rattles toward the buffalo chip and sing this song.

More than a hundred buffalo
Have gathered near.
More than a hundred buffalo,
Waiting to feed your people.

After I had learned the words, I stood on the ground and looked toward the buffalo chip. I began shaking the rattles and sang the song aloud.

Without warning, something butted me from behind. It bent my knees, and down I fell. The rattles scattered in the grass. I jumped up and grabbed my bow and arrow. The bow was drawn when I whirled around. Instead of an enemy, there stood a small buffalo calf!

"Hello, Little Yellow Buffalo," I said. "Did you hear my song? You are young to be such a yellow color. Where is your mother? What will you do when I ride away? You will be all alone."

When I rode into our camp, my mother and father saw Little Yellow Buffalo following me.

My mother and father knew the stone was real and that I would have the power to find and call the buffalo for our people. My father also remembered a visit from Spider God. Now he understood. He began to seek the holy man's help in my training to be a buffalo caller and in making a Beaver Bundle.

Little Yellow Buffalo provided my baby sister with a special robe. My mother tanned his skin with the

hair intact. The robe was warm and
very beautiful.

When I prayed to the buffalo
stone, I asked Little Yellow Buffalo
to protect my baby sister.

Three

The Rope

As seasons marched by, the need for grass and water kept buffalo herds on the move most of the time. Winter bachelor days turned into summer running season. The bulls joined the cows. From late summer to early fall, the buffalo grouped together in small and large herds. Grass was at its plentiful best. The buffalo became big and fat. Late fall was the best time for tribal hunting. Baby calves were born in the spring.

There were many kinds and sizes of buffalo. The qualities of their hides varied with the seasons. The color of their coats varied with their ages.

The buffalo was a very big animal, yet easily frightened. A sudden movement, sound, or unusual odor could cause buffalo herds to stampede. The passing shadow of a cloud or the sight or smell of man could send them running. Careful and strict rules governed the hunts.

There were many lessons to learn. Special songs were sung to make the buffalo approach our camp. The holy man taught me mystic rites to perform. He also taught me to watch for a raven flying in a circle over our camp. "You must caw to the raven," he said. "The raven will answer by flying off in the direction of the nearest herd of buffalo."

When our fathers and uncles
went on an early fall hunt, my friends
and I grabbed our bows and arrows,
jumped on our horses and met at the
doorway of our village. We knew
that when the hunters gave chase, the

cows abandoned their calves. The cows ran first. The bulls ran behind the cows. The calves brought up the rear. A large number of deserted calves were left on the hunting ground.

These calves gave us a chance for a miniature chase. We rode into the middle of them making all the noise we could make. They scattered this way and that. We gave chase!

Racing over rough ground that was riddled with bushes, rocks, and hidden burrows caused me to spill one day in the middle of a chase!

I rolled in the dirt and grass. Away ran Blaze. I felt much like a buffalo calf. I dashed out of the way of a pony. I dodged a raging calf. The dust was choking! It blinded me! There was no escape. Suddenly, a thundering noise came toward me. There was nothing I could do. Then a familiar hand wrapped around my arm and jerked me up behind a rider. My father had saved me!

The next day my father said, "Come. It is time you learned to use that long rope you made."

Father tied my rope around his horse's neck. He let its free end drag the ground. He jumped on his horse and raced away. Suddenly he fell off. Quick as a wink, he grabbed the rope that was trailing on the ground.

Father's horse came to a sharp stop. In a flash, Father was back on his horse racing back to me.

"Train Blaze to do that, Ahiga," Father said. "Practice. You must act fast to grab the rope."

"Don't worry, Father!" I said. "I will!"

Four

Blackfeet Facts

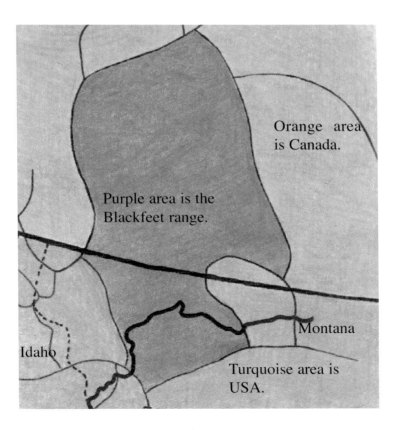

Orange area is Canada.

Purple area is the Blackfeet range.

Montana

Idaho

Turquoise area is USA.

Four different decoration styles of the Blackfeet tepees. They really lived in their tepees year round and some of them were very large. They had separate liners that they could attach to the inside of the poles, too, to give them an extra layer of protection. The decorations symbolized sacred emblems and animals, but were sometimes also just for beauty.

Hunters would paint their faces and wear the robes of wolves as they trailed the buffalo, slipping through the tall grass, almost invisible. The buffalo knew the wolf smell and did not pay it much mind. It was the human smell that would stir them up. Wearing the wolf skins, the hunters could approach within several feet of the buffalo sometimes for a good clear shot.

There are places in the Blackfeet range in southern Canada where great buffalo jumps are still visible. Some have been protected as parks. The people made great heaps of stone along a path that narrowed as it reached the cliffs. Then many men would circle a small herd and drive it toward the cliffs. This was more common before they had horses, but even after, it was an effective method. People behind the piles of stone would yell and wave branches to keep the buffalo from turning away and the drivers would force the animals to the edge of the cliff. They were butchered at the bottom. There are huge areas of artifacts left at these slaughter sites.

Examples of Blackfeet beadwork: Moccasins, gauntlets and vest. The northern tribes were very skilled at making gloves, and the big flaps that flared back over the wrists both protected the arm and, in cold weather, over-lapped their clothing for more warmth.

 Left is an ammonite that the Blackfeet called the Buffalo stone and held sacred as having mystical powers. It is said that these rare and beautiful fossilized shells sing a music that certain people can hear. They were kept in the medicine bundle of whoever found one. These fossils are only found in a small portion of the Blackfeet range. They are considered gemstones today and are made into necklaces and rings. Their color rivals that of the fire opal.

Milky Way

Beyond "The End"

● Telling stories was popular with the Blackfeet, as with all Native American tribes. Storytellers told stories about the tribe's past, to explain religious beliefs, or to pass on their values. Children were told many stories. They kept them in their memory to share with their own children. Fairy tales we tell begin with "once upon a time". Blackfeet stories often begin with "before the people came". Ask your parents to tell you a story about your grandparents when they were young. Then tell the story to your class.

37

CURRICULUM CONNECTIONS

● In what state is the Blackfeet Reservation? If you want to write to someone your age at the reservation, the address is: Blackfeet Tribe; P.O. Box 850; Browning, MT 59417.

● A buffalo calf weighs up to 40 pounds when it is born. How much more does a buffalo calf weigh than you weighed when you were born? Borrow the school nurse's scales. Weigh your classmates until their total weights equal 40 pounds!

● Learn something about the language of the Blackfeet at <www.angelfire.com/ar/waakomimm/lang9.html>. Learn to say the name of your birthday month. What is the name of the present month?

● July is a good time to see the Milky Way. Three bright stars in the Summer Triangle, high in the eastern sky, serve as a guide to the Milky Way. The light from one of those stars, Altair, that you saw in July 2003, started on its journey to Earth in 1986! How many light-years away is Altair?

● This was a game Ahiga might have played to develop hunting skills: Ring Toss. Attach a hoop to a stick with rawhide (string). Use a small hoop for older children and a larger hoop for small children. Start with the hoop laying flat on the ground. Swing the hoop upward. Try to put the end of the stick through the hoop!

THE ARTS

● The buffalo was life to the Plains Indians. A major part of the Blackfeet's life was centered in and around the buffalo herds. Boys were taught that when the robe hunters rode into a herd in January or February, they looked for the four-year-old buffalo. Their coats of hair were fluffed out, silky, and thick, like fine fur. They were the best of all hides.

As a class project, make a papier mache buffalo. You might want to begin with a buffalo shape made from chicken wire, then apply the papier mache. There are recipes for papier mache at website <www.homeschoolzone.com/pp/crafts/papermache.htm>

GATHERING INFORMATION

● While gathering information about the Blackfeet Nation, we found references about things women did besides the domestic chores. This is an exciting part of gathering information—when unexpected things pop up.

The sacred buffalo stone is a major object of the Blackfeet. The first one was found by a woman. The Sun Dance, an important tribal ritual, was led by an aged medicine woman. The most fascinating story was about a female warrior named Running Eagle. She is famous for her bravery and celebrated for her war deeds. Read about it at <www.meyna.com/ppiegan.html>.

41

THE BEST I CAN BE

● *"What is life? It is the flash of a firefly in the night. It is the breath of a buffalo in the wintertime. It is the little shadow which runs across the grass and loses itself in the sunset."*

Think about these words of wisdom, spoken by Chief Crowfoot. Make an effort for your flash of light to make life better for others. May your breath in the wintertime be from words that are pleasing to others. Be sure that your shadow that runs across the grass makes the world a better place.

Remember to always BE THE BEST YOU CAN BE!